How the Cow Jumped Over the Moon

Sally Huss

ISBN: 0692317376
ISBN 13: 9780692317372

In an endless field of green grass a cow stood chewing her cud...

…when a frog hopped up. "What's new? What's new with you?" asked the frog.

"I'm tired. I'm bored," said the cow. "I chew and chew. I stay in this pasture. That's all I do."

"It's a lovely day," said the frog. "Why don't you hop along with me? There's a lot to see."

"No! No!" said the cow. "I don't know how."

"Rrribit. Rrribit" said the frog. "Try something new."

"I couldn't do that," said the cow. "I chew and chew. That's all I do."

"Too bad for you," said the frog, as he flipped and skipped, and went on his way to enjoy the day.

Then a dog wandered by and asked the cow, "What's new? What's new with you?"

"Nothing" said the cow. "I'm tired and bored. I chew and chew. I stay in this pasture. That's all I do."

"Well, come with me. I'm going to swim in the pond. It's over the hill, a little beyond."

"No! No!" said the cow. "I don't know how."

"Bow, wow," barked the dog. "Try something new."

"I couldn't do that," said the cow. "I chew and chew. That's all I do."

"Too bad for you," said the dog, as he jumped and sprang on his way to enjoy the day.

With that a pig waddled by. She asked the cow, "What's new? What's new with you?"

"Nothing," said the cow. "I'm tired and bored. I chew and chew. I stay in this pasture. That's all I do."

"Join me in a mud bath," invited the pig. "I know a very nice hollow in which we could wallow."

"No! No!" said the cow. "I don't know how."

"Oink! Oink!" said the pig. "Try something new."

"I couldn't do that," said the cow. "I chew and chew. That's all I do."

"Too bad for you," said the pig, as she danced and twirled…

… and went on her way to enjoy the day.

Then a horse galloped up and asked the cow, "What's new? What's new with you?"

"Nothing," said the cow. "I'm tired and bored. I chew and chew. I stay in this pasture. That's all I do."

"How about a race up the hill? There's a tree full of apples. I'm sure it's there still."

"No. No," said the cow. "I don't know how."

"Whineeee! Whineeee!" bellowed the horse. "Try something new."

"I couldn't do that," said the cow. "I chew and chew. That's all I do."

"Too bad for you," said the horse. He kicked up his heels, swished his tail and went on his way to enjoy the day.

Nighttime was approaching and on and on the cow chewed.

Finally, a chicken stopped by and asked, "What's new? What's new with you?"

"Nothing," said the cow. "I'm tired and bored. I chew and chew. I stay in this pasture. That's all I do."

"Join me," invited the chicken. "I'm going to jump over the moon."

"No! No!" said the cow. "I don't know how."

"Forget that! No excuses," said the chicken. "I'm going to show you how. First, you've got to want to do it. Then try and try and never stop until you do, do it. Watch me," she said…

… and up she flew, over a few clouds and stars into a sky of dark blue.

The cow was amazed.

Well, she thought, it would be something new. If a chicken could do it, she could too.

Then she thought about it, decided she wanted to do it, and set her mind to it.

Then she jumped and jumped and never stopped...

… until finally the cow jumped over the moon.

In the background a little dog laughed to see such a sight and fish ran away with a raccoon.

From that time on the cow was never bored because, as she chewed and chewed, she would dream up something new to do… and then she'd do it!

The end, but not the end of trying something new.

What do you think the cow is dreaming up to do? What can you dream up to do that you'd like to do?

Are you going to take anyone along, like your friends or family, when you do what you'd like to do?

You might take some paper and draw some of the things you'd like to do and draw the people or animals you would like to take along.

***

At the end of this book you will find a Certificate of Merit that may be issued to any child who has made great strides in the areas stated in the Certificate. This fine Certificate will easily fit into a 5"x7" frame, and happily suit any child who receives it!

Here is another fun, rhyming book by Sally Huss.

When a loon, a baboon, and a raccoon complain that they are too close to each other, they move apart. But then they seem to be invading the territory of the local cows, which in turn find them too close. The three move away again, this time to a pond with a school of boorish Moorish idols that are also unwelcoming. They find relief on an island, but that too has inhabitants who insist that they move on. So it goes until the three are surprised by a butterfly who changes their thinking. Perhaps getting along with each other might just be a good idea.

GETTING ALONG WITH EACH OTHER – http://amzn.com/B00JPV4W90.

If you liked HOW THE COW JUMPED OVER THE MOON, please be kind enough to post a short review on Amazon: http://amzn.com/B004WOWQXY.

Sally creates new books all the time. If you would like to be alerted when one of her new books becomes available and also when one of her books is offered FREE on Amazon, sign up for her newsletter here: http://www.sallyhuss.com/kids-books.html.

More Sally Huss books may be viewed on the Author's Profile on Amazon. Here is that URL: http://amzn.to/VpR7B8.

About the Author/Illustrator

Sally Huss

"Bright and happy," "light and whimsical" have been the catch phrases attached to the writings and art of Sally Huss for over 30 years. Sweet images dance across all of Sally's creations, whether in the form of children's books, paintings, wallpaper, ceramics, baby bibs, purses, clothing, or her King Features syndicated newspaper panel "Happy Musings."

Sally creates children's books to uplift the lives of children and hopes you will join her in this effort by helping spread her happy messages.

Sally is a graduate of USC with a degree in Fine Art and through the years has had 26 of her own licensed art galleries throughout the world.

This certificate may be cut out, framed, and presented
to any child who has demonstrated her or his worthiness to receive it.

Certificate of Merit

_____
(Name)

The child named above is awarded this Certificate of Merit
for being adventurous and persistent in:

*Trying new things
*Sticking with what has been started
*Completing tasks

Presented by: _____ Date: _____

Made in the USA
Coppell, TX
30 November 2020